Dear Parents:

Congratulations! Your child is taking the first steps on an exciting journey. The destination? Independent reading!

STEP INTO READING® will help your child get there. The program offers five steps to reading success. Each step includes fun stories and colorful art or photographs. In addition to original fiction and books with favorite characters, there are Step into Reading Non-Fiction Readers, Phonics Readers and Boxed Sets, Sticker Readers, and Comic Readers—a complete literacy program with something to interest every child.

Learning to Read, Step by Step!

Ready to Read   Preschool–Kindergarten
• big type and easy words • rhyme and rhythm • picture clues
For children who know the alphabet and are eager to begin reading.

Reading with Help   Preschool–Grade 1
• basic vocabulary • short sentences • simple stories
For children who recognize familiar words and sound out new words with help.

Reading on Your Own   Grades 1–3
• engaging characters • easy-to-follow plots • popular topics
For children who are ready to read on their own.

Reading Paragraphs   Grades 2–3
• challenging vocabulary • short paragraphs • exciting stories
For newly independent readers who read simple sentences with confidence.

Ready for Chapters   Grades 2–4
• chapters • longer paragraphs • full-color art
For children who want to take the plunge into chapter books but still like colorful pictures.

STEP INTO READING® is designed to give every child a successful reading experience. The grade levels are only guides; children will progress through the steps at their own speed, developing confidence in their reading. The F&P Text Level on the back cover serves as another tool to help you choose the right book for your child.

Remember, a lifetime love of reading starts with a single step!

Visit us on the Web!
StepIntoReading.com
randomhousekids.com

Educators and librarians, for a variety of teaching tools, visit us at
RHTeachersLibrarians.com

Library of Congress Cataloging-in-Publication Data
Depken, Kristen L.
The shy little kitten / by Adam McKeown ; illustrated by Sue DiCicco.
pages cm. — (Step into reading. Step 1)
Adapted from the 1946 Little Golden Book "The shy little kitten," written by Cathleen Schurr; illustrated by Gustaf Tenggren.
Summary: When a mother cat leads her kittens into the barnyard sunshine, one kitten lingers behind and embarks on an adventure, meeting a variety of animals along the way.
ISBN 978-0-553-49763-2 (trade) — ISBN 978-0-375-97377-2 (glb) — ISBN 978-0-553-53720-8 (ebook)
1. Kittens—Juvenile fiction. [1. Cats—Fiction. 2. Animals—Infancy—Fiction.
3. Animals—Fiction.] I. DiCicco, Sue, illustrator. II. Schurr, Cathleen. Shy little kitten. III. Title.
PZ10.3.D425Sh 2015
[E]—dc23
2014029290

Printed in the United States of America
10 9 8 7 6 5 4 3 2 1

This book has been officially leveled by using the F&P Text Level Gradient™ Leveling System.

THE SHY LITTLE KITTEN

Adapted from the beloved Little Golden Book
written by Cathleen Schurr and illustrated by Gustaf Tenggren

By Kristen Depken
Illustrated by Sue DiCicco

Random House 🏠 New York

One mama cat.

Six little kittens.

Black-and-white.

One has stripes.

Down the ladder.

Jump, jump, jump!

Onto the grass.
Roll, roll, roll!

The little striped kitten

is very shy.

Pop!

A chubby mole!

They go
for a walk.

Green frog.

Big mouth!

The mole and the kitten
laugh and laugh.

Bounce, bounce!
A shaggy puppy!

Where is the mama cat?
The shaggy puppy knows!

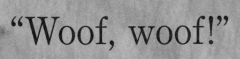

"Woof, woof!"

A red squirrel!

"Chee, chee, chee!"

Down the hill.

Hop, hop, hop!

Across the brook.

Onto the farm.

Mama cat!

One, two, three, four, five, six little kittens.

Picnic time
on the farm!

Seeds for the chickens
and ducks.

Carrots for the rabbits.

Mash for the pigs.

Berries and milk
for the little
kittens!

Uh-oh.

PLOP!

SPLASH!

All the animals
laugh and laugh.

Best day ever!